WELCOME TO
PASSPORT TO READING
A beginning reader's ticket to a brand-new world!

Every book in this program is designed to build read-along and read-alone skills, level by level, through engaging and enriching stories. As the reader turns each page, he or she will become more confident with new vocabulary, sight words, and comprehension.

These PASSPORT TO READING levels will help you choose the perfect book for every reader.

READING TOGETHER
Read short words in simple sentence structures together to begin a reader's journey.

READING OUT LOUD
Encourage developing readers to sound out words in more complex stories with simple vocabulary.

READING INDEPENDENTLY
Newly independent readers gain confidence reading more complex sentences with higher word counts.

READY TO READ MORE
Readers prepare for chapter books with fewer illustrations and longer paragraphs.

This book features sight words from the educator-supported Dolch Sight Words List. This encourages the reader to recognize commonly used vocabulary words, increasing reading speed and fluency.

For more information, please visit passporttoreadingbooks.com.

Enjoy the journey!

Little, Brown and Company

Hachette Book Group
1290 Avenue of the Americas, New York, NY 10104
Visit us at lb-kids.com

Little, Brown and Company is a division of Hachette Book Group, Inc.
The Little, Brown name and logo are trademarks of Hachette Book Group, Inc.

The publisher is not responsible for websites (or their content) that are not owned by the publisher.

First Edition: May 2015

ISBN 978-0-316-29992-3

10 9 8 7 6 5 4

CW

Printed in the United States of America

Passport to Reading titles are leveled by independent reviewers applying the standards developed by Irene Fountas and Gay Su Pinnell in *Matching Books to Readers: Using Leveled Books in Guided Reading*, Heinemann, 1999.

minionsmovie.com

MINIONS

Who's the Boss?

by Lucy Rosen

LITTLE, BROWN AND COMPANY
New York Boston

Attention, Minions fans!
Look for these words when you read
this book. Can you spot them all?

T. rex

caveman

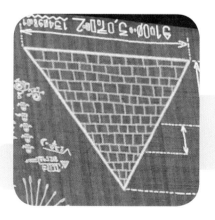

pyramids

banana

See these funny yellow creatures?
They are called Minions.
Minions are small and round.
They go by many names,
like Dave, Paul, Carl, and Mike.

Each Minion is different,
but they all share the same goal:
to serve the most despicable master
they can find.

Minions have wandered the earth
for millions of years,
searching for the perfect villain
to be their master.

Masters were not hard to find,
but they were hard to keep.
Something always went wrong.

First there was the T. rex.

The Minions followed
the mighty beast as he stomped
through the forest.

They scratched his back.

They scrubbed his head.

They sent him flying
into a volcano by mistake.
"Whoops!" said the Minions.

Next came the caveman.
The Minions helped him
fight off wild animals.

Well, most of the time.

Minions have served some of the greatest leaders in history.
Or they have tried to, at least.

They built the pyramids in Egypt, but they built them upside down. This caused the pyramids to fall... right on top of the pharaoh.

Then the Minions made Dracula
their master, until they accidentally
turned him into dust.

The Minions moved
from one evil villain to another.
They never seemed to find
their perfect fit.

Once, they stood by one of the world's
fiercest and shortest generals.
It turned out that Minions
do not make very good soldiers.

The Minions did not give up hope,
no matter how often they failed.
And they failed a lot.

Finally, after being chased away
by the little general's army,
the Minions built a new home.
It was big enough for the whole tribe.

The Minions were safe.

They were secure.

They had everything

they could need.

But still, something was not right.
Without a bad guy to serve,
they had no purpose.

They became sad and aimless.
The Minions did not know
what to do.

But all was not lost,
for one Minion had a plan.
His name was Kevin.

Kevin would leave the cave
and not return until he found
his tribe the biggest, baddest
villain to serve!
But he needed help.
"Buddies," said Kevin.
"Kiday come me!"

"Me coming!" said Bob,
the littlest Minion.
He was ready to help.
From the back of the room,
another hand went up.

Stuart had been volunteered by
his friends while he was napping.
And so the three Minion heroes
got ready for their journey.

Kevin felt pride.

He would be the one to save his tribe.

Stuart felt hungry.

He would be the one to eat this banana.

And Bob?

Bob was scared of the journey ahead.

But as long as they stuck together,

Bob knew everything would be okay.

"Let's go!" cried the three
Minion friends.
It was time to find
a new despicable master!